DADDIES

DADDIES

ADELE ARON GREENSPUN

PHILOMEL BOOKS

New York

This book is
FOR MY FATHER, SAMUEL ARON 1906–1950
and
for my readers whose fathers
may live only in dreams and wishes.

Once I was a daughter. Sam's daughter. It is hard for me to write these names. Father. Daughter. Sam.

In the summers when our family went to the seashore, it was my father who held my hand as we waded into the roaring ocean. I tightened my grip when its strong tide pulled us, and the sand washed away from our toes. Together we waited for the waves, and he would pick me up just in time to miss being knocked over. I liked best when he carried me on his shoulders into the deep part where the water was over my head, beyond where the breakers began. It was there he would teach me how to float on the calm ocean.

My father taught me how to ride a bicycle. Holding the bar under the seat, he ran by my side as I learned to balance. One day he stopped running, and I kept riding, and two blocks later when I realized he was no longer there, I fell off. We always laughed when he told the story.

My father told me bedtime stories about when he was a little boy.

My father was patient when he helped me with math homework. He knew how to explain word problems so I would understand them.

My father bought me a wagon of blocks when my brother was born. They became castles and towers and cities and hours of fantasy.

My father taught me how to bind my sixth-grade project into a book. I had drawn pictures and written text about the daily lives of the ancient Egyptians. He must have been proud of me. My teacher showed the book to the principal, the other teachers, and everyone who visited our classroom.

My father called me Petunia. His flower. He made me feel special. When he looked at me I knew he loved me.

When I was eleven years old, my father died. Suddenly. He had been in the hospital only a few short weeks, and in the early morning hours on the day before the Fourth of July, he died. My mother did not tell me. At noon that same day, her sister, Aunt Leah, put me on a Greyhound bus. She telephoned my mother from the depot and passed the phone to me. "How's Daddy?" I asked. "The same," she replied. I heard tears in her voice. Aunt Leah didn't tell me either. A trunk mysteriously packed with my clothes was slid into the bin under the bus before it left for the Pocono Mountains. Camp was to be my home for the summer.

Each day I wrote letters to my father about camp, about the laps I swam to earn a Red Cross badge, my part in the musical show, the blue box I made for him in arts and crafts.

When other campers received letters from their parents, I told myself my father was too sick to write.

One weekend, four weeks later, my mother appeared at camp. She said, "Daddy went away," but her face told me "died." My daddy died.

I saw him walk away and disappear beyond where the water meets the sky. Now I would no longer have someone to take me into the deep ocean, and I became afraid to go to dangerous places without a hand to hold.

My father remained fixed in a perfect light. He never had the chance to embarrass me, argue with me about boyfriends or curfews or politics, or just be wrong.

The weekend following my mother's visit, there was a special event. Parents' Day. I stood with my bunkmates who happily awaited their parents' arrival. Listening for the crush of gravel beneath the wheels of my father's blue and grey Pontiac, I waited for him to drive through the stone gates. He would carry cookies and candy in brown shopping bags, just like the fathers who were walking up the hill toward the bunk, with arms around their daughters. I wished I could have asked the other girls' fathers if they would be my father for the day, if they would look at me the way my father used to look at me. No one came.

The blue box I had made for my father, the one I would never be able to give to him, lay on a shelf inside the arts and crafts studio. I had sanded the wood and painted it blue, with white curlicue designs and little red hearts which circled the names *Sam* and *Eva*. I couldn't give it to my mother either; I was afraid it would make her sad. I felt stupid to have made a gift for someone who was already dead, so I shoved the box deep in my cubby.

This book brings the blue box back as though I were still holding its weight in my hands. I see the bright colors, feel its square shape, and smell the wood.

I try to remember a gift I gave my father during his life. A pasted birthday card? A wide tie? Purple socks? Nothing.

Now I read the poem I wrote for this book, and the words surprise me.

> Daddies need
> hugs and kisses,
> smiles and tickles,
> jokes and giggles,
> funny faces, and
> "I love you."

I had given him something after all. The pleasures and joys I created without knowing, the invisible ones, the ones which enriched his life.

Daddies is the blue box I was never able to give to my father. I give it now to you.

ADELE ARON GREENSPUN

DADDIES

Daddies

hold babies,

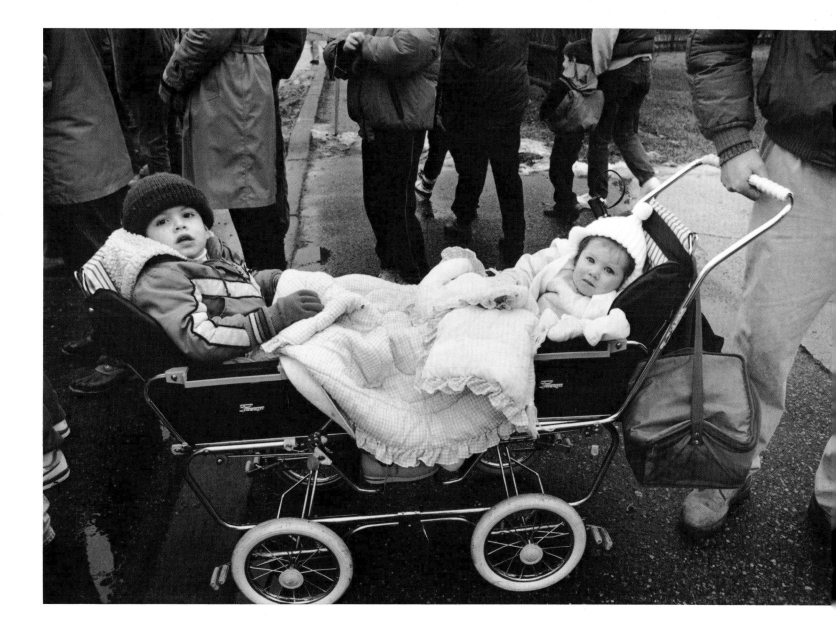

push strollers,

share
feelings,

read stories.

Daddies have
shoulders to stand on,

bellies to sit on,

backs to climb on,

hands to hold.

Daddies give hugs

and kisses,

tickles and giggles,

piggyback rides.

Daddies
teach

how to

swim,

and dive,

ski,

catch

and throw,

win,

and lose.

Daddies take us

to parades,

and
home again,

on picnics,

to parties,

to the zoo.

Daddies
need

hugs and kisses,

smiles

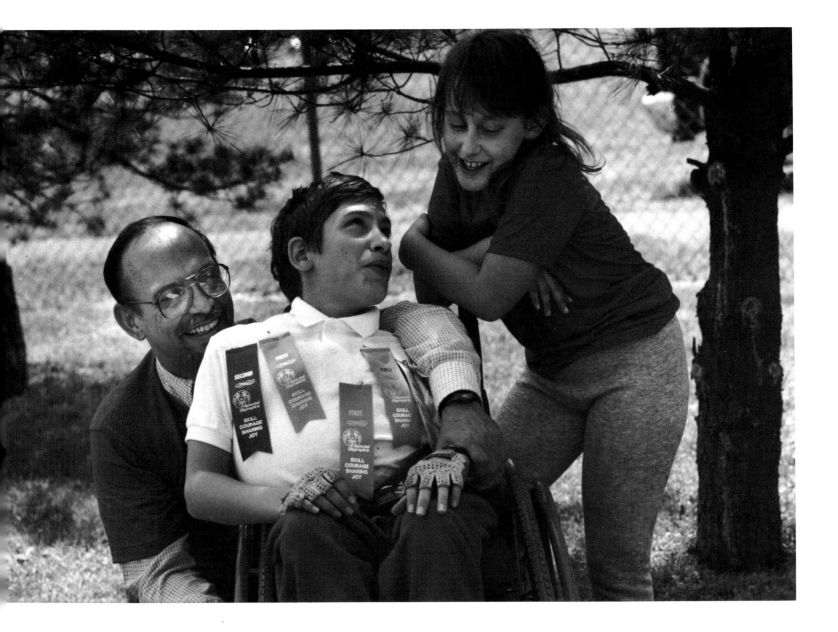

and
tickles,

jokes

and giggles, and

"I love

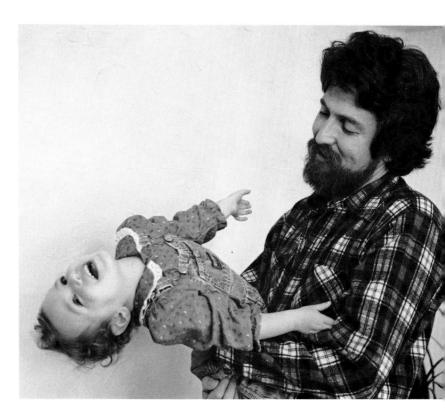

you."

Philomel Books, a division of The Putnam & Grosset Book Group,
200 Madison Avenue, New York, NY 10016.
Published simultaneously in Canada.
Printed in the United States.
Book design by Kathleen Westray

Library of Congress Cataloging-in-Publication Data
Greenspun, Adele Aron.
Daddies / Adele Aron Greenspun. p.   cm.
Summary: Text and photographs depict all the special things fathers do.
ISBN 0-399-22259-6 :
1. Fathers — Juvenile literature.   2. Father and child — Juvenile literature.
[1. Fathers. 2. Father and child.]   I. Title.
HQ756.G76   1991   306.874'2 — dc20   90-15578 CIP AC

First Impression